Timmie in London

Timmie in London

by Vivian Werner

Illustrated by Elise Piquet

Doubleday & Company, Inc., Garden City, New York

For Margot
and Ivor
and Mark

Chapters

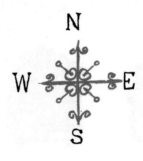

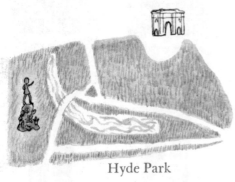

Hyde Park

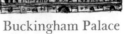

Buckingham Palace

Science Museum

TO GUILDFORD, 30 miles

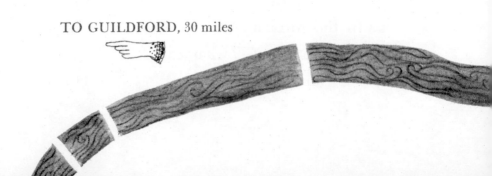

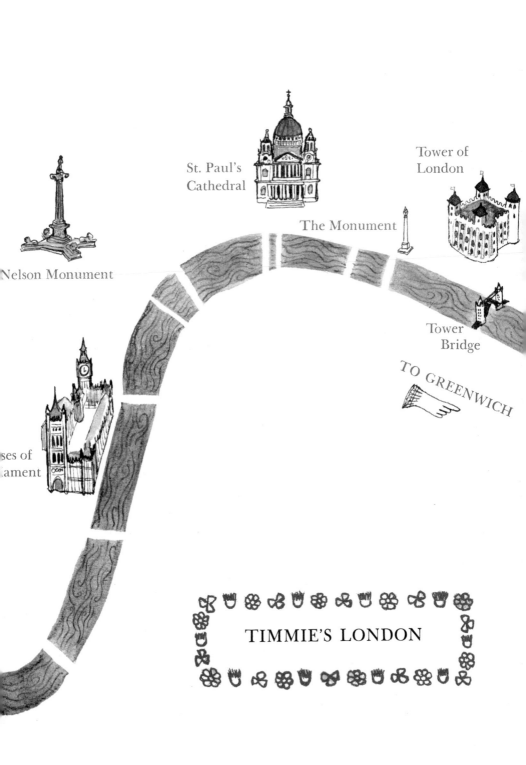

St. Paul's
Cathedral

Tower of
London

The Monument

Nelson Monument

Tower
Bridge

TO GREENWICH

ses of
ament

TIMMIE'S LONDON

1

...in London

"London Bridge is falling down, falling down, falling down . . ." Timmie sang. "London Bridge is falling down . . ."

It was a song Timmie hadn't sung since he'd been in nursery school. That had been five or six years ago, when Timmie was very small. Since then Timmie had hardly even *thought* about the song.

But Timmie sang it now for a very special reason. Timmie was in London!

And maybe, Timmie thought, he could see London Bridge. Maybe he could see it now, from the window of the hotel.

It was such an exciting idea that Timmie popped upright in the carved wooden bed with the light quilt that was as warm as the sand at the seashore, and as fluffy as fresh snow. It was such an exciting idea that Timmie dropped to the floor without putting on his slippers, although it was very cold.

He hurried across to the window and peeped through it. Outside, everything was dim and hazy, as if the whole world had been caught between the dark and the daylight.

Timmie stepped back, to make sure the window shade wasn't drawn. But the cord and tassel hung high above him. Timmie decided the window must be very dirty.

He wiped it with the sleeve of his pajamas.

But that didn't make any difference. When Timmie peered out the window again, the whole world seemed covered with a silvery, shimmering curtain of tiny beads that Timmie recognized at last as fog.

Through it, Timmie could see the houses across the way, and the street in front, too. Everything glimmered and glistened. The houses seemed to come nearer and nearer to Timmie, and then to run away as if they were frightened, getting smaller and smaller. And then, not frightened at all, the buildings and the street came nearer, just the way Timmie's own face had, once, when he'd stood on the bridge back home and looked at himself in the river.

Then the buildings across the way, and the street, too, stopped quivering and shivering and stood stock-still, as the sun came up behind them. It seeped through the fog and lit up the buildings, turning them a gleaming white.

Timmie stared out, looking this way and that. In front of the hotel, behind an iron fence, was a patch of green. It seemed to grow and grow until it became a park that stretched as far as Timmie could see.

But Timmie couldn't see London Bridge, even when he climbed on a chair. He decided to ask Daddy where it was.

Timmie dressed himself quickly. Then he found Daddy. "I can't see London Bridge," he said.

"You won't be able to from here," Daddy told him. "It's too far away." Then, when he saw how disappointed Timmie looked, he said, "But we could go there."

"Right away?" Timmie asked.

Daddy looked at his watch. "We could go as soon as we've had breakfast," he said.

Timmie wasn't really hungry. He knew, though, that Mother would want him to eat at least a little breakfast, because mothers always do, so he didn't say anything.

They went down to the dining room in what Timmie would have called "the elevator" back home, but which he had already learned was called "the lift" in England.

Great, huge paintings hung on the walls of the dining room. Some were of bearded men wearing beautiful velvet suits, and some were of ladies with beautiful velvet dresses and stiff-starched ruffles at

their throats. Daddy told Timmie they were kings and queens of England who had lived a long time ago.

Some were very good kings and queens, who had made England rich and prosperous, and some had led the British in times of war. And one King, Henry VIII, hadn't really been good at all. He had quarreled with his ministers, and with the bishops of the Church, and had had six different wives and terrible table manners.

When the waitress brought *his* breakfast, Timmie, of course, ate it very nicely. He ate broiled kidneys

and mushrooms, an egg, and a large broiled tomato, while Mother and Daddy were eating a kind of smoked fish called "kippers."

He drank a large glass of milk. Then he helped himself to a piece of freshly buttered toast that stood up straight in the silver toast rack. The toast was cut into triangles, and Timmie spread a piece with a thick layer of bitter marmalade.

Timmie and Mother and Daddy all had another piece of toast. Then Timmie got his raincoat and Daddy got *his* raincoat, and Mother got *both* her raincoat and her umbrella. And the three of them went outside, down the wide, scrubbed steps of the hotel, to the street.

Timmie stopped to look around at the big buildings of brick and stone, at the park in front of the hotel, at the row of houses on the other side. London suddenly seemed so large that Timmie was a little bit frightened. Quickly, he slipped his hand into Daddy's.

He was glad he did. Because a black car came rolling down the street, on the wrong side of the road.

At first Timmie thought that the driver had made a mistake.

But another car came along, and that was on the wrong side of the street, too. And then a whole stream of cars came along . . . and they were *all* being driven down the wrong side of the street.

Just then Timmie noticed that the cars themselves were different. They had steering wheels on the wrong side of the car, way over on the right, instead of the left like all the other cars Timmie had ever seen.

Timmie was just going to ask about it when Daddy said, "Here comes our bus!"

Timmie looked down the street quickly, the way he would at home, for the bus. But, of course, it wasn't coming that way. It was coming *up* the street.

Timmie turned around just as it drew up beside them. Then he sucked in his breath, because it was a great big one that looked like *two* buses, one on top of the other, and it was painted a bright, shiny, fire-engine red.

The bus stopped. Timmie hopped on and scampered up the narrow, winding staircase to the top. He went straight to the front seat.

Mother and Daddy came upstairs, too. Then the man who had helped them on the bus came upstairs and down the aisle. "Fares, please," he called. "Fares, please."

When he stopped in front of Daddy, Daddy said, "London Bridge."

"Three and six," the man said.

Timmie tugged on Daddy's arm. "What does 'three and six' mean?" he asked.

"It means three shillings and sixpence, Tim," Daddy explained.

"Sixpence," Timmie said. It reminded him of something he had heard a long, long time ago. So many things in London reminded him of things he had heard long, long ago.

And then he remembered. "Sing a song of six-

pence . . ." Timmie began. It was another song he had learned in nursery school. " 'Sing a song of sixpence . . .' What *is* sixpence?" he asked.

Daddy fished a small silver coin from his pocket and gave it to Timmie. It wasn't much bigger than a dime. "That's sixpence, Tim," he said.

He gave Timmie another coin. It was made of cop-

per and it was as big as a silver dollar. "That's a penny, Tim," Daddy told him.

Then Daddy gave Timmie a *smaller* copper coin. "That's a halfpenny," he said. "But you call it 'ha'penny' or 'hay-p'ney.'"

Daddy took one more piece of money from his pocket. It was a yellowish color, with an edge that was uneven, like the circles Timmie had cut out of paper to hang on the Christmas tree when he had been very small, before he had learned to cut properly. "This is a 'thrup'ney' bit," Daddy said.

Timmie held all the coins in his hand. "That's a funny name!" he said. And then he made up a little poem. "Funny money." He was so pleased with the poem that he said it over. "Funny money!"

But it would be so difficult to remember all about English money that he slipped the coins into his pocket and stared out the window.

The bus rolled past enormous buildings made of white stone, street after street of them. Timmie thought he had never been in such a big city.

And then, as they went around a circle,

Timmie saw a man standing in the middle of the street directing traffic. He looked like the policeman back home who helped Timmie cross the street every morning when he went to school. Just like Officer Perkins, he was wearing a neat blue uniform.

But on his head he wore a hat that looked like a water pail, maybe, or a coal bucket turned upside down.

Timmie was so excited he pointed right at the man, although he knew that wasn't at all polite.

Just then Mother saw the policeman, too. "Look, Timmie," she said. "There's a bobby!"

Timmie stared at the bobby until the bus turned the corner. Then he stared at the buildings again, and at the people they passed.

All the men seemed to be wearing black bowler hats that were round as melons cut in half. They all wore gloves, and they all carried umbrellas, and they strode along as if they were very, very busy.

The streets got narrower and wound in and out. At last the bus came to a lovely tall white column. There was a tiny platform near the top of it, and from the platform flew the British flag.

"We're almost at the Bridge," Daddy said. "That's the Monument that was put up a long time ago. It shows where the terrible fire started . . . oh, four hundred years ago . . . that burned down much of London."

"But the Bridge didn't burn, did it?" Timmie asked.

"Not the Bridge," Daddy said. "But there were houses on London Bridge in those days, and a lot of them burned down."

Then Daddy said that *this* bridge was only a hundred and fifty years old. But there had been another bridge, at this same place, that had stood for six hundred and fifty years.

There had been bridges before that, too. The first had been built by the Romans. Later, other people had built bridges there, and settled near by. Sometimes London Bridge had fallen down. But another was always built to replace it.

Because of the bridge, a town grew around it. And the town grew into one of the largest cities in the world, London.

The bus went on a little farther. Then they all scrambled down the stairs and jumped off. And there they were, right at the beginning of London Bridge!

Daddy took Timmie's hand, and Timmie took Mother's. And the three of them walked over the Bridge, to the center of it.

They stopped there and looked up the river, to the part of London they had come from. The big buildings were spread out as far as Timmie could see.

Then they looked the other way.

They could see another bridge, the Tower Bridge, which had enormous stone turrets at each end.

While they watched, the bridge between the towers opened in the middle, and each side rose straight in the air. A shiny-scrubbed boat sailed through the

open bridge. Beyond it, Timmie saw lots and lots of other shiny boats, floating on the river.

When the boat sailed on, and the bridge had been lowered, Timmie and Mother and Daddy walked *back* over London Bridge.

They had only gone a few steps before Timmie stopped.

He started to jump . . . up and down, up and down, up and down.

Nothing happened.

This bridge didn't move or shake or tremble. It didn't even wiggle.

Timmie ran ahead. When he caught up with Mother and Daddy, he was singing, "London Bridge is falling down, falling down, falling down."

Timmie knew it wasn't, of course.

Timmie knew that now it was only a song.

2

Buckingham Palace

Timmie hopped down the stairs of the hotel.

He jumped around and hopped back up.

He started to hop down again. Just then, a tiny gray kitten poked her head around the bottom step.

Timmie ran down the steps right away. He stooped down and patted the kitten. "Pussy cat, pussy cat, where have you been?" he asked.

The kitten could only say, "Me-ow."

But Timmie knew the rest. "I've been to London to see the Queen," he finished for the kitten.

That gave Timmie an idea. He picked up the kitten and rushed into the hotel, looking for Mother and Daddy.

Mother was very surprised when she saw what Timmie had in his arms. "What have you there?" she asked.

Timmie was quite sure Mother could see it was a kitten. Still he said, "It's a kitten." Then he asked, "Mother, can we go and see the Queen?"

Mother was even more surprised. But Daddy understood.

"I don't think we can see the Queen," he said. "But we could go down to Buckingham Palace, where the Queen lives, and see the Changing of the Guard."

It was such a wonderful idea that Timmie let the kitten go and clapped his hands.

The kitten sat on the floor and looked at Timmie as if she wanted to be picked up again. Timmie hardly noticed. Instead, he held his arms very stiff, just the way soldiers do . . . and the way he was sure the Guards would do . . . and marched around the room.

Then he marched off to his room. He got his coat and put it on.

When he came marching back, Mother and Daddy were ready to go, too. So Timmie picked up the kitten from the chair where she had gone to sleep, curled up and purring gently. He carried her outside and left her just where he'd found her.

Daddy hailed a taxi, but it was Timmie who said, "Buckingham Palace, please," in a loud, clear voice. Then they all climbed in and drove off through London.

They passed big square buildings with tall columns in front. They passed rows and rows of houses, all alike. They passed little parks with iron railings around them, where boys and girls were playing.

Then they came to a very big park, with a lake

inside it. There were ducks swimming on the lake, and swans and geese, too.

At the end of the park, they drove around a circle that had a huge marble statue of one of England's greatest queens, Queen Victoria. And there, beyond the circle, and behind a *very* tall fence, was the biggest building Timmie had seen in London.

It was long and low, with large round columns, too, like the other buildings they had passed. And it had millions and trillions and zillions of tall windows . . . well, anyway, it had a lot of windows that sparkled in the sun. And the flag that meant

that the Queen was there that very day was flying proudly above it. And over the doorway there were lions carved in stone.

There were lions, too, on the gates that were so tall Timmie had to tilt his head back to see the tops of them. *These* lions stood on their back legs, looking *very* ferocious. Timmie was sure that if they'd been real, they would have roared so that everyone in London would have heard them, and even Timmie would have been afraid.

But he wasn't afraid now, and he went right up to the gate.

And there, near the doors of the Palace, standing stock-still in front of two tiny wooden houses, were the Guards.

They wore beautiful red coats and black trousers with red stripes down them. On their heads they had tall black fur hats made of bearskin, that were held on with gold straps across their chins. And each held a rifle in his white-gloved hand.

The hats were so big that Timmie could hardly see the faces of the Guards, and they came down so low over their foreheads that Timmie wondered if the Guards could see *him*.

And they didn't move. Timmie watched and watched and the Guards just stood there.

Then, all at once, one of them thumped his rifle on the ground . . . three times . . . just like that. He picked it up and shifted it from one hand to the other. He thumped again. Then he put the rifle across his other shoulder and walked out in front of his house, marching stiffly, the way Timmie had marched that morning.

Standing in front of his house, the Guard stamped his feet three times. Then he turned and walked to the great doorway at the center of the Palace. And before he turned and marched back, he stamped his feet again.

And at that very moment, the other Guard did the
same thing. He thumped his rifle and stamped his
feet, and then *he* marched to the Palace door and
back.

Then, right together, the *two* Guards stamped and
thumped and marched to the door and back.

They stamped their feet again . . . But just then,
Timmie heard the sound of horses' hoofs.

He turned around quickly . . . Timmie didn't bother to stamp *his* feet . . . and there, coming down the road, were more Guards.

They wore beautiful red coats, too. But over their coats they wore glimmering, golden armor. On their heads, they wore spiked, golden helmets, with thick golden tassels. Each of them held a gleaming sword in his hand. And each of them sat straight and proud on a beautiful black horse.

They rode straight past Buckingham Palace, to-

ward another palace. They would guard it most of the day, sitting tall on their horses, and *they* wouldn't move at all.

The Horse Guards were barely out of sight when Timmie heard the sound of drums, faint and far away. Soon he heard the sound of fifes, too.

The music grew louder and louder.

And then Timmie saw them all! Lots and lots of Guards, not on horses, but on foot. They stepped smartly along, swinging their arms all together. The

drummers were drumming and the pipers were piping and everyone marched in time to the music.

They went around the statue and across the wide road. Then the big gate in front of the Palace was opened. The Guards marched through the gates and formed a circle near the Palace. And everyone stood straight and still while the Fife and Drum Corps played another tune.

Before they had even finished, another band came down the street. This was a big band, with bright brass trumpets and glistening horns. Ahead of the band marched a Guard carrying a flag that floated in the breeze, and another Guard with his sword held high. And a whole regiment marched behind it, right around one side of the statue and into the Palace courtyard.

And then . . .

And then!

Another regiment came marching around the *other* side of the statue.

At the head of *this* regiment was a big, gray, shaggy dog.

He was an Irish wolfhound, because these were the Irish Guards, and the dog was their mascot. He marched proudly along, with his head held high, keeping time to the music just like the Guards.

And behind *these* Guards came the Irish Pipers.

They didn't wear red tunics and bearskin hats. They didn't wear black trousers with a red stripe down them.

They didn't wear trousers at all!

The Irish Pipers wore short brown kilts that looked like skirts, and green tunics with silver buttons. They wore knee socks, too, like the boys Timmie had seen playing in the parks. And on their heads they had dark green berets, with blue plumes sticking up.

At the head of the Irish Pipers marched three men with drums that went rat-a-tat-tat . . . rat-a-tat-tat. But the others, who marched behind the drummers, all carried bagpipes!

The Irish Pipers marched into the courtyard, too. And when they formed a circle there, it was right in front of Timmie.

After the big band stopped, the Irish Pipers played. And when they had finished, the Guards lined up facing each other. The officers stepped forward, and the Guards with the flags marched back and forth, and everyone else saluted.

Then the bands played again. When they had all finished, the Guards turned and marched away.

The last to go were the Irish Pipers, with the big shaggy dog leading them again.

Timmie and Mother and Daddy waited until everyone else had gone. The music faded away in the distance. Only two Guards were left. They stood stock-still in front of the little houses, as they had when Timmie and Mother and Daddy had first seen Buckingham Palace.

3

The Tower of London

Timmie got up and got dressed very early.

No one else in the hotel was awake except, of course, the maid. She brought cups of tea to people when they rang for her, almost as soon as they opened their eyes.

Timmie tiptoed down the stairs and through the lobby. He went outdoors.

The sun was just coming up and the air was cool

and fresh. Timmie stood at the top of the steps and took a deep breath.

He would have liked to play in the little park across the street. But the park was kept locked, and the hotel clerk who had the key was still asleep.

So Timmie sat down on the top step and waited.

Before long, the little kitten tiptoed past.

"Here kitty, kitty, kitty," Timmie called.

The kitten pattered up the steps, and Timmie picked her up.

Then the two of them . . . Timmie and the kitten . . . sat there on the top step and waited.

Soon Timmie heard the rumble of wheels, and then he saw a man in a jacket and a long striped apron coming down the street, pulling a cart behind him. There were rows and rows of bottles on the cart. The large ones were filled with milk, and the medium-sized ones were filled with milk, too. And the little ones were filled with cream.

Timmie hurried down the steps, still holding the kitten.

"Please," he called to the man, "could I have some cream?"

"Certainly," the man said.

"It isn't really for *me*," Timmie said. "It's for my kitten." He tucked her under one arm. Then he dug into his pocket and found the coins Daddy had given him. He held them all out to the man . . . the six-pence piece, and the threepenny bit and the penny and the ha'penny. "Will that be enough?" he asked.

The man looked at the coins and then at the kit-ten and then at Timmie. His eyes twinkled. "I think this will be enough," he said, taking the penny. "Since it's for your kitten."

Timmie put the other coins back in his pocket. The man gave him the cream, and Timmie said, "Thank you," very politely. He climbed the stairs and sat down again.

Timmie opened the cream. The kitten lapped at it daintily. When she had had enough, she wiped her

whiskers clean with her pink tongue, curled up in Timmie's lap, and fell asleep.

Another milk cart clattered past.

This one wasn't any bigger than the first had been. But the milkman wasn't pulling this one. He was standing up inside it, at the front, and driving.

Like the other cart, this one was red, a beautiful bright red . . . just like the buses Timmie had ridden on. And just like the coats of the Guards that Timmie had seen.

Timmie wished he might have a coat like theirs.

He wished he might *be* a Guard.

And he wished the kitten were a big, shaggy gray dog . . . an Irish wolfhound . . . instead of a kitten.

Just then the kitten woke up. She yawned and stretched, and then went back to sleep. *She* was quite content to be a kitten.

Timmie put her down gently, and went back into the hotel. Daddy was sitting in the lobby, drinking tea, and smoking a pipe.

"Daddy," Timmie said, "could we see the Guards again? They had *such* beautiful uniforms," he added wistfully.

"We could," Daddy said. "But if it's uniforms you want to see, Tim, maybe we should go to the Tower of London."

Daddy puffed on his pipe. Timmie thought about the Tower of London. He thought about Buckingham Palace, too. He didn't see how any uniform could be more wonderful than the ones the Guards wore. Still . . .

Daddy blew a smoke ring. It hung over Timmie's head before it floated away. "They might have some Guards at the Tower, too," Daddy said.

Timmie made up his mind very quickly. "Let's go to the Tower," he said. So Timmie and Mother and Daddy went to the Tower of London.

And the Tower of London wasn't really a tower at all!

It was a marvelous castle, like the ones Timmie built in the sand when he went to the beach.

It wasn't made of sand, of course, but of rough gray stones that would last forever. And all around the castle were thick walls, because the Tower had once been a fortress.

Inside the walls, though, there were towers everywhere, and of every size and shape. There were tall ones and small ones. There were thin ones and fat ones. There were even flat ones!

The tower Timmie liked best was called the White Tower. It was the biggest of them, and it stood in the center of them all, at the top of the hill.

The White Tower had rounded domes with slim, short spires, and lacy-looking arrows that turned with the wind because they were weather vanes, and lacy-looking crowns above them because the Tower of London belonged to the Queen. And rippling in the breeze, high above the White Tower, was the British flag.

There *was* a Guard, too, but there were so many other things to see, Timmy hardly noticed him.

Timmie looked straight ahead while they crossed a small bridge and walked under an arch between two square towers that were as much alike as twins. He looked from side to side as they started to cross a *big* bridge.

But at the center of the big bridge, Timmie looked *down*. And right beneath him was a moat!

Long ago, when kings and queens had lived in the castle, the moat had been filled with water. And when other kings and queens, or even noblemen, had tried to attack them, they had raised the drawbridge which had been right where Timmie stood now. No one had been able to enter the Tower, then, and the king or queen had been safe behind the thick walls.

At the other end of the bridge, Timmie and Mother and Daddy walked under an arch between *round* twin towers that were part of the wall itself. They passed a tall tower with a belfry perched on top. It wasn't in the middle, though, like the one in the steeple of the church at home where Timmie went on Sundays. This belfry was over at the edge, where it looked as if it would topple off at any moment.

They went on to a large round tower that was guarded by a man in the most marvelous suit Timmie had ever seen.

It wasn't really a suit, though. It was more like a dress made of dark blue wool that the man wore over dark blue trousers.

The dress came down to the man's knees. It had a wide belt, and full sleeves, and little cuffs and a tight collar that stood up straight. The man wore a dark blue hat, too, that looked a lot like a very big cake on a very small plate.

And everything was trimmed in red!

There were bands of red on the front of the dress and on the sleeves, the belt and the hat. And across the man's chest were the enormous red initials *"E.R."* with the number *"II"* between them. Daddy said they stood for *"Elizabeth Regina,"* the Latin words for "Queen Elizabeth," and that the *"II"* meant she was the second Queen Elizabeth to have ruled over England.

Timmie was so delighted, he could only say "Oh!"

While they climbed the stone steps of the tower, Daddy told Timmie all about the guard. He was a Yeoman Warder, Daddy said, but most people called him a "Beefeater."

Timmie thought that was a funny name for some-one who wore such a fancy costume. "Do the Beef-eaters always dress like that?" he wanted to know.

Daddy shook his head. "Those are just their every-day clothes," he said.

If those were just their everyday clothes, Timmie wondered what they would wear when they got dressed up.

"They wear scarlet outfits, trimmed with gold," Daddy said. "And they wear high, starched ruffles at their throats, like the queens in the paintings in

the hotel. They wear knee breeches, too, and scarlet stockings. But their shoes are black, and so are their hats, and both are trimmed with ribbons. And they always wear white gloves."

Timmie thought that Beefeaters dressed like that would be the most wonderful sight in the world . . . until he reached the top of the tower and saw what was in it. *That,* Timmie decided, was the most wonderful sight in the world!

In the center of the round room was a round glass case filled with beautiful crowns of real gold and purple velvet and white ermine. All the crowns were

studded with jewels . . . with diamonds and sapphires and emeralds . . . that seemed to flash with fire so bright it made Timmie blink.

There were swords, too.

There were gleaming swords of gold, with diamonds as big as Timmie's hand . . . well, almost . . . set into the handles. There were other swords that sparkled with pearls and rubies. Timmie could just imagine kings dressed in golden armor riding forth on white horses, with these very swords in their hands.

They would have been very brave kings, who

fought huge dragons that belched flames and roared so that they could be heard through all the land. And of course the king would have killed the dragon, because that was what kings were for . . . to protect the people they ruled over.

And there were scepters!

Timmie could imagine a strong, handsome follower of the king kneeling before the throne. The king would have tapped him on the shoulder with one of the scepters and made him a knight, because he would have fought the dragon as bravely as the king.

Timmie could even imagine what it must have been like, to have lived in a castle like this. "Daddy," he asked suddenly, "did little boys ever live in the Tower?"

"Once upon a time," Daddy said, as if it were a fairy tale, although Timmie knew that *this* had *really* happened, "once upon a time, long, long ago, two little Princes lived here. The Tower was used as a prison in those days. The little Princes were shut up in the Tower by their cruel uncle, who wanted to be king himself. And he had the little Princes murdered."

Timmie thought it was very sad about the Princes. He asked if he could see where they had lived. So he and Mother and Daddy went to another tower.

They climbed a tiny, winding staircase that was very dark. Instead of windows, there were only narrow slits in the walls, where soldiers had shot out arrows, in the days when the Tower had been a fortress.

The rooms that Timmie and Mother and Daddy went through were very dark, too, and very gloomy, with walls of stone and doors of heavy, paneled wood.

The gloomiest of all was the room where the little Princes had lived.

In the very middle of that room, Timmie discovered a book. It was a history of the world, and it had been written by another prisoner who had been held captive in this very same place. His name was Sir Walter Raleigh.

Timmie knew about him, because Sir Walter had been an explorer, as well as a writer. And he had sailed to America, long before he had been made prisoner, and had founded one of the first colonies there.

The colony had disappeared. No one ever knew for sure what had happened to the people Sir Walter had left behind him. But people knew where the colony had stood, and Timmie had studied about it, in his history book.

Then, because it was all so sad, Mother suggested that they go to see the armor. "But not the old armor in the White Tower that knights used to wear," Mother said. "The other armor."

Timmie asked Daddy what other kind of armor there was.

But Daddy wouldn't tell him. All he said was, "You'll see!"

"Is it horses' armor, Daddy?" he asked.

"You'll see," Daddy said again.

They opened the door . . . and then Timmie understood!

Standing in front of the door, as if to guard it, was a great gray stuffed elephant with gleaming ivory tusks. *And the great gray stuffed elephant with gleaming ivory tusks was wearing shining silver armor!*

It was made of little squares, like the patchwork quilt on Timmie's bed. Like Timmie's quilt, some of the squares were plain, and some had flowers on them and *some* squares had *elephants* on them.

Mother and Daddy went all around the room, looking at swords and spears and lances, at daggers and sabers and scimitars. But Timmie stood in front of the elephant until it was time to leave. And all the time he stood there, he was imagining that he was

riding right on top of the elephant, plunging into
battle, or crashing through deep jungles.

Timmie thought about the elephant all the way
back to the hotel. The little kitten was waiting for
him, just outside the hotel. He walked right past her.
He wished she were an elephant.

Timmie thought about the elephant when he went to bed, too.

And then he thought about the little Princes. He was very sorry for them, because it was so sad.

He pulled the blankets over his head, and closed his eyes very tight. He wished Mother would come into his room.

Just then, Timmie heard a faint scratching outside, and then a soft "Me-ow." He opened the door and the kitten came padding into the room. She jumped up on Timmie's bed. Then she curled up on Timmie's pillow and fell fast asleep.

Timmie climbed back into bed himself.

He was glad, now, that the kitten wasn't an elephant.

He was glad she wasn't even an Irish wolfhound.

He was quite content to have the kitten just a kitten.

4

Out to Guildford...

When Timmie woke up, the kitten was sitting at the foot of his bed. She cocked her head to one side, as if to say, "Sleepy head, sleepy head! Come on, come on . . . Get out of bed!"

So Timmie popped up and hopped up . . . and just then the kitten scurried to the door. She waited there, as if to say, *this* time, "When, oh *when* do I get my breakfast?"

Timmie dressed very quickly. He picked up the kitten and carried her downstairs.

Just as they went outdoors, Timmie saw the milk-man turn the corner. And just as he had done the day before, Timmie called out, "Please, could I have some cream?"

And . . . as he had done the day before, the milk-man said, "Certainly!"

So Timmie gave the man a penny again, and the man gave Timmie the cream, and Timmie gave the cream to the kitten.

The kitten lapped up all she wanted. Then she curled up in Timmie's lap and went to sleep.

Timmie waited on the top step until the second milkman came down the street. He waited until a man came by pushing a little cart ahead of him, and sweeping the street with a long-handled broom. He waited until the postman came by with his packet of letters.

Timmie patted the kitten. He was glad she was a kitten. Still, it would have been nice to know someone in London he could talk to. It would have been nice to know another boy.

Timmie sighed. He put the kitten down and went back into the hotel. It was breakfast time. Timmie was hungry so he went into the dining room.

Mother and Daddy were waiting for him there. Timmie climbed onto the big square wooden chair, with the high back that was all carved in whirls and swirls and curlicues.

jersey

He unfolded his linen napkin. In England, Timmie knew, it wasn't called a napkin at all, but a "serviette." And a truck wasn't a truck. It was a "lorry." And when you wanted tooth paste or a tooth brush or medicine, you didn't go to the drug store . . . you went to the "chemist's."

Wellingtons

Timmie was thinking how strange it was when Daddy asked, "Do you like London, Tim?"

"Oh yes," Timmie said.

"You aren't lonely here, are you?" Mother wanted to know.

biscuits

"Well . . . a little," Timmie admitted.

"Then maybe you'd like to meet Andrew," Daddy suggested. "He's an English boy."

dressing gown

pram

Timmie said, "Oh yes!" Then he asked, "Does Andrew live in London?"

Daddy shook his head. Then he smiled. "No," he said, "he lives in Guildford."

Timmie was puzzled. "But that's where *we* live."

Daddy shook his head again. Then he explained that the Guildford Andrew lived in was very near London. It was in England, of course, and not in New England, which was the part of America Timmie lived in.

But over three hundred years ago the people who lived in Andrew's Guildford had come to America, and had founded a town there. It was called Guilford, for the town they had come from. Like the Pilgrims, who had landed at Plymouth Rock, they had left England to find a place where they could worship as they pleased.

The people who had come from Andrew's Guildford had built the very house that Timmie and his

mother and daddy lived in now. They had built the church where Timmie went to Sunday school, and they had cleared the trees away to make the village Green that Timmie crossed every day on his way to school.

The people of Guildford and the people of Guilford had spoken the same language then. And they still did . . . almost.

The families had had the very same names. And they still did. And the people of Guildford and the people of Guilford had lived by laws that were almost alike. Although there were some things the early settlers hadn't liked about England, they believed that English laws were fair and just. So they had copied them.

Later, when the American colonies had fought the Revolution against the King of England, they still kept their respect for the English belief in liberty. So they had modeled their own Constitution, and especially that part called the "Bill of Rights," on something called "the Magna Charta."

That had been an agreement made between King John and the English barons, way back in 1215. By signing it, John admitted that all government had to be according to law, and that no one, not even a king, could break that law. A king couldn't plunder or rob or murder, any more than a peasant could. John admitted, too, that the king had the duty to protect his subjects by seeing that the laws were enforced. And the barons agreed that it was their duty to be loyal to the king and to fight for him.

The Magna Charta was important, too, because in it, King John *guaranteed* to the English people the liberties they already had and granted them other

liberties, besides. He promised that they would be free to speak as they chose, even if they said they didn't like what the king was doing. He pledged that they would *remain* free, and that no one would be put to death, or sent to prison, or have his property taken away from him, unless he had had a fair trial by jury. All these things, Daddy told Timmie, had been put into the American Constitution.

Timmie knew about the Pilgrims, of course, because his teacher had told Timmie's class about them at Thanksgiving time. And he knew about the American Revolution because every year, on the Fourth of July, Timmie watched the fireworks that were set off to celebrate the signing of the Declaration of Independence.

But there were a lot of things Daddy told Timmie that he *didn't* know. Timmie wanted to hear more, but Daddy said, "Well, Tim, if we're going to meet Andrew, we'll have to hurry."

"Is Andrew coming to London?" Timmie asked.

"No," Daddy said. "I thought we might all go out to Guildford. That is, if you'd like to."

"*I'd* like to," Timmie said. "Oh, Daddy! Can we?"

"I'll see," Daddy said. "I'll ring them." That was what the English said when they wanted to telephone.

Daddy went out. Timmie was just finishing breakfast when he came back. "What do you think, Tim?" Daddy said. "Andrew's mother and daddy have invited us to tea."

Timmie thought that was smashing . . . something he'd heard someone say, here in London. But he didn't tell Daddy that. He just got his coat.

When they got to Guildford, Andrew's mother and daddy were waiting for them. And so was Andrew.

He was just as big as Timmie, and just as old. But he wasn't dressed like Timmie.

Andrew wasn't wearing long trousers. Andrew was wearing short blue ones. He was wearing woolen socks that came to his knees. And Andrew was wear-

ing a blue blazer with silver buttons, and a striped cap . . . *and* a red and blue striped necktie. On his blazer was a big, bright emblem, the insignia of Andrew's school.

Andrew shook hands politely with Timmie. "How do you do?" he said.

Timmie said, "How do you do?" too. But he couldn't think of anything else to say.

They all walked through the town.

Timmie couldn't think of anything to say.

They stopped in front of a red brick building that might have been a castle. It had turrets topped by rounded domes and weather vanes, like those in storybooks.

The windows were very big, but they were made of such tiny panes of glass that Timmie wondered how anyone could see through them.

The carved wooden door was open. When Timmie and Andrew peeped through the doorway, they saw a man standing on a tiny patch of lawn, like the Green back home, only smaller.

But the man wasn't dressed like anyone back home, or like anyone Timmie had ever seen. He wore a bright blue gown, and a funny flat cap, both made of the cloth for which Guildford was once famous.

And his costume showed that he took care of the old and sick people who lived in the building.

They walked down a street paved with old cobblestones, then. On both sides of it were storybook houses. Some were of brick and some were of smooth white stucco. Most of them had high, pointed roofs, as steep and sharp as the spikes of the white picket fence around Timmie's house. And most of them had enormous windows that jutted out over the street.

But the most marvelous building wasn't really a house. It was the Guildhall, which was like the Town Hall back home.

It didn't look like Timmie's Town Hall, though. Timmie's Town Hall was very plain.

But the Guildhall had a beautiful balcony, with carved wooden beams. It had big windows, with tiny, leaded panes. It had a bell tower, with a rounded top which it wore like a hat.

And it had a clock that hung way out over the street!

The clock was black and gold, and it was held to the building by iron, spotted with gold, too, and as delicate as lace. When Timmie saw it, he just stared. He couldn't think of *anything* to say!

65

At the end of the street, they turned a corner. They passed very old houses, small and square, with small windows. They went under a very, *very* old arch and right up to a big brick house with a fence around it.

It looked like an ordinary house, but Timmie was sure it was magic, because of the sign on the fence. On it were pictures of Alice in Wonderland and the Cheshire Cat and Tweedledum . . . or was it Tweedledee? And this was the house where Lewis Carroll, who had written *Alice in Wonderland,* had lived.

After that, they all went to Andrew's house. Timmie and Andrew went outdoors, to the neat back yard with the flower beds around it. And at each end of the yard, Timmie saw three sticks driven into the ground. There were bits of wood across the tops, and Andrew said they were wickets and were for a game called cricket. The three sticks were called stumps, and the pieces across the top, bails.

Andrew found a flat bat, then, and a heavy ball, and showed Timmie how to play. He threw the ball, keeping his arm very straight and very stiff, and tried to make the bits of wood fall. Timmie stood in front of the wicket and tried to keep the ball away by hitting it with the bat. When he did, he scurried to the other wicket and scored a run . . . just like baseball!

Then it was Andrew's turn to bat. And he scored a run, too.

After Andrew and Timmie had scored a lot more runs, they sat down on the steps, and Andrew told Timmie more about cricket.

In real matches, Andrew explained, there were two sides, each with eleven players. They all wore chalk-white flannel trousers and sweaters. Most

matches lasted two days. But *Test* matches, when a team from another country played an English team, lasted five or six days. The men played for six hours each day, stopping only for lunch and tea.

Andrew had hardly said "tea" when his mother called them in. "Tea is ready," she said.

So Timmie and Andrew sat at a small table set just for them. On it were plates of raisin bread and nut bread, sliced as thin as Mother's sugar cookies. And all the bread was nicely buttered.

There were scones, too. And pots of marmalade, honey and jam and meat pastes that Timmie and Andrew spread on everything.

After they'd eaten the bread and the scones, they had something called "trifle." It was cake that had been spread with jam and then with custard, and *then* covered with cream. Andrew liked it so much, he clapped his hands when he saw it.

With the bread and scones and trifle, Timmie and Andrew drank rich, cool milk . . . they didn't drink any tea.

Timmie didn't say anything while they ate. He didn't say anything because he was too busy eating.

After, when Mother and Daddy and Andrew's mother and daddy had *their* tea, and Timmie and

Andrew sat on the steps again, Timmie didn't say anything, either. He was too tired.

Still, when they left, and when Andrew said, "Thank you for coming," Timmie remembered to answer, "Thank you for having me," the way boys and girls in England always did.

They went back to London on a bus. And when they got to the hotel, Timmie went right to bed. When Daddy came in to say good night he asked, "What did you think of Guildford, Tim?"

Even though Timmie was very, *very* sleepy, he knew exactly what to say.

"I think it's smashing," Timmie said.

5

...and Down to Greenwich

When Daddy went shopping and bought suits and shoes and an umbrella in a place called "Bond Street," Timmie went, too. He helped Daddy carry home his packages.

When Mother shopped in a marvelous outdoor market that had all sorts of things, like Grandmother's attic, Timmie went, too. When Mother bought old glassware and a gleaming silver teapot and two silver candlesticks, Timmie carried home the candlesticks.

And when Mother and Daddy took Timmie shopping . . . well, there were so many packages Mother had them sent. There were the sweaters that the saleslady called "jerseys." There were boxes of books. And there were sets and sets of little lead soldiers. Some were Crusaders and some were Roman gladiators. And some were Irish Guards, like the Guards at Buckingham Palace.

One day Daddy looked at all the boxes and bags and bundles. "I *really* don't know how we'll get all this home," he said, "unless we go by boat!"

Timmie dropped a Guardsman on the floor. "Oh, let's!" he said.

Daddy laughed, "Would you like to go on a boat today, Tim? Just a little boat?" he asked.

"I'd like to go on *any* kind of boat," Timmie said.

"There's one that goes down the Thames to Greenwich," Daddy told him. "Maybe Andrew can go, too. I'll see if he can meet us."

Andrew was already waiting when Timmie and Mother and Daddy reached the pier. He stood beside a boat that bumped and bobbed and floated about. Daddy bought tickets, and they all went aboard.

Just as they sat down, the big clock in the tower

behind them struck twelve. The motors coughed and sputtered. The man in the cabin spun the big wheel, and the little boat churned and turned and chugged out into the middle of the river.

From there, of course, Timmie could see the huge buildings that Daddy called the Houses of Parliament. But he could see the lampposts, too, with the bronze dolphins twined around them, that stood straight among the trees on top of the embankment. And he could even see the bronze heads of lions, with the

bronze rings held in their snarling jaws, set into the
stone wall along the river.

Along both banks of the Thames, Timmie and Andrew saw enormous buildings. Some were very old
and some were very new. Some were tall, like the
skyscrapers Timmie had seen in New York. Some
were long and low, like the palaces Timmie had
seen in London. Some were not so long or wide or
tall, but had points and peaks and poles on them.
And one wonderful building, the London fish mar-

ket, even had golden dolphins for weather vanes!

Sometimes there were spires and domes and steeples rising among the buildings. Most of them, Daddy said, were on churches designed by Sir Christopher Wren. He was born over three hundred years ago, and during most of his long life . . . he had lived over ninety years . . . he had been the greatest architect in England. That was why he was asked to plan so many buildings, after the terrible London fire. That was why he had designed the monument to the fire, too.

And all the way down the river were the bridges. Some were plain, ordinary bridges that were old and drab. Some were new and spick-and-span. Some were only for trains, and some were for cars and the big red buses, and for people, too.

Just before they reached London Bridge, Daddy pointed to the shore. "Over there is where the Globe Theater once stood," he said. "No one knows *exactly* where, because it burned down so long ago. But that was where many of Shakespeare's plays were first performed, nearly four hundred years ago."

Then Daddy said, "Look, Tim. There's the Tower of London . . ."

But Timmie was busy looking at the boats.

Everywhere Timmie looked, he saw boats.

There were sight-seeing boats, like the one Timmie and Andrew were on. There were tankers carrying oil, and there were flat barges carrying coal. There were freighters with cargoes of lumber and grain.

There were tiny boats that skimmed the surface of the water. There were tugs that moved slowly, as if they were tired. There were battleships, and frigates used by the British Navy to train sailors. There were great ocean liners, freshly painted, with rows and rows of portholes and fat, striped smoke stacks.

There was a beautiful yacht which belonged to the Queen.

Anchored next to the yacht was a sailing ship.

When Timmie asked Daddy what a sailing ship was doing in the Thames, Daddy explained that it was the *Discovery,* the ship on which Captain Scott had sailed to the Antarctic, when he explored the South Pole.

Then Daddy said, "Captain Scott was the first Englishman to reach the South Pole. But he never came back. So the ship is a memorial to him."

When Timmie saw people on the deck of the *Discovery,* he wanted to go on board, too. But Daddy said, "Not today, Tim. Today we'll go on the *Cutty Sark!*"

Before long, they saw *her*, too . . . a graceful, wooden ship with three masts that stood tall and proud, and with rigging that looked as tangled as Mother's knitting after the kitten had played with the ball of wool.

When their own boat pulled up to the dock in Greenwich, Timmie and Andrew jumped ashore. They rushed over to the *Cutty Sark,* the clipper ship which had first set sail almost a hundred years ago. It was the only one still left.

As soon as Mother and Daddy reached the gang-plank, everyone went on board. Then Timmie and Andrew explored the fo'c'sle. The crew had slept *there.*

They explored the galley, where meals had been cooked on an old iron stove. They peeked into the deckhouse where the apprentices had slept on hard bunks that were so narrow Timmie was sure they must have fallen out when the ship rocked. They clambered down staircases as steep as ladders, and climbed back up them. They looked into the captain's wood-paneled cabin. They stood near the big steering wheel, and felt the cool breeze blowing on their faces, like real sailors. And they went below and inspected the cargo, as the captain himself must once have done.

There were chests of tea, stored where they were when the *Cutty Sark* had sailed back from China. And there were bales of wool, too, like those she had carried home from Australia.

When they had made certain everything was in order . . . like a real captain . . . Timmie and Andrew went on deck. Mother and Daddy were waiting for them. And Mother said, "How would you like to see the Museum? Everything in it is connected with English sailors, or with English ships."

The Museum was in a low white building with lots and lots of columns. It stood in a beautiful park. But Timmie and Andrew hardly noticed *that*. What *they* noticed was the big anchor in front of the building. And the red flag, with more anchors on it, which flew from a ship's mast, instead of a flagstaff.

The anchor was big, and the flag was, too. But when they went into the Museum, they went straight to a room filled with models of ships. And *they* were very small.

There were sailing ships and whaling ships. There were steam ships and ships that people pushed along with poles and other ships that people had to row.

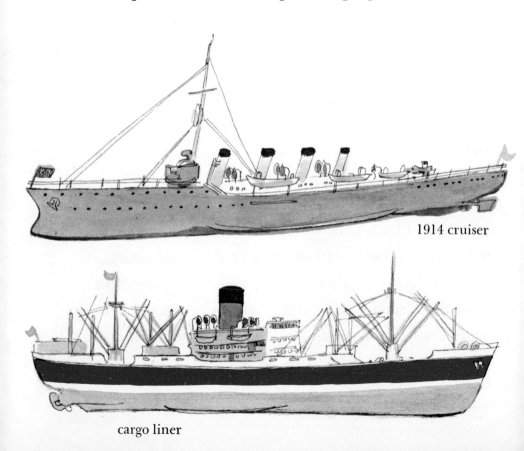

1914 cruiser

cargo liner

There were great modern liners . . . like those that crossed the ocean. And there were warships.

Some of the warships were the kind that Timmie had seen, sailing down the Thames. But the ones that Timmie liked best were the models of those that had been used hundreds and hundreds of years ago.

Some were made of wood, and others had been carved of ivory, or of bone. Some were in full sail, and from the masts floated silk flags, no bigger than Timmie's thumb.

And on the decks were cannon as small as matchsticks. They were carved of wood or bone or ivory, too. And they were so real Timmie was sure people

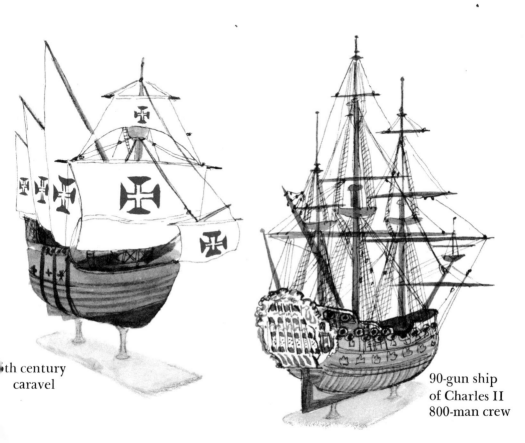

th century
caravel

90-gun ship
of Charles II
800-man crew

could shoot them, if they could only find cannon balls small enough.

Some of the ships had tiny anchors, and some had golden lanterns, and golden wreaths around the portholes. One even had little men, carved in wood, and painted gold, across the bow. And at the tip of the boat was a figurehead . . . a tiny gold knight on horseback. Timmie stared at it until Andrew said, "Let's see the barges!"

Timmie really didn't want to see the barges. He had seen barges on the Thames, and they were all black or dingy brown, and not at all splendid, like the little boats. But he wanted to be polite to Andrew, so he followed him into the next room.

And when Timmie saw *these* barges, he took a deep breath and held it almost forever.

These were the royal barges. And these barges were painted marvelous colors like scarlet or blue. And they were decorated with gold, like the models, even though they weren't models, but real barges that kings and queens had ridden in, long ago.

After they saw the barges, Timmie and Andrew and Mother and Daddy saw the figureheads. They were real, too, like the uniforms they saw, and the swords and guns.

Finally they left the Museum and walked back to

the little boat tied up at the pier. When they got on board, Timmie sat on the open deck. The bright sunlight flashed across the water. The man started the motor and the boat chugged out into the Thames.

As they sailed along, everything seemed to change. The boat wasn't a little launch, with wooden benches around it for people like Timmie and Andrew.

The boat had turned into a royal barge, all scarlet and gold.

And Timmie wasn't sitting under a piece of tarpaulin.

He was sitting on blue velvet cushions, in a golden cabin that was guarded by golden lions and decorated with golden dolphins.

6

In the Museum

Timmie and Andrew stood with their faces pressed against the window. They watched the rain that splashed against the glass and trickled down it in little rivers.

Timmie sighed. Andrew had come in all the way from Guildford to spend the day with him. He wondered what they would do. "Rain, rain, go away . . ." he began.

". . . Timmie and Andrew want to play," Andrew finished.

The rain didn't pay any attention. Not to Timmie and not to Andrew. It just came down steadily.

So Timmie and Andrew stared out the window. They didn't even turn around when Mother and Daddy came in. They didn't even turn around when Daddy asked, "What is it, Tim?"

Timmie simply said, "It's raining."

Andrew said it, too. "It's raining."

Daddy looked out the window. "It certainly is."

And Mother said, "Oh, dear! Whatever shall we do today?"

"We can't go walking," Timmie said.

And Andrew said, "We can't go to the zoo."

"No," Daddy said, "we can't. But we could go to a museum."

"We could go to the British Museum," Andrew said.

Timmie thought the zoo might be a lot more fun than the Museum. But since they couldn't go to one, he asked Daddy, "What do they have there?"

Andrew answered, even before Daddy could. "They have mummies," he said.

Timmie looked at Daddy. "That's right," he said. "They have mummies there."

Then he explained that mummies were the bodies of the "Pharaohs," the kings of Egypt who had lived over four thousand years ago, and of their queens. Some, though, were the bodies of the dogs and cats that had been their pets.

And some were the bodies of beetles, because the Egyptians had considered them sacred.

All the bodies had been preserved with rare spices and strange ointments. Then they'd been wrapped in bandages and put into beautiful painted wooden cases.

Now the mummies in their wooden cases were in the Museum.

It seemed to Timmie that the Museum might be as much fun as the zoo. Still, he wondered what else they had there.

When he asked Daddy, Andrew said, "They have toys."

Timmie looked at Daddy again. And again Daddy said, "That's right." Then

he explained that the toys were kept in glass cases, because they were only to look at, now. But they were real toys that boys and girls had played with nearly two thousand years ago, in Rome or in Athens.

"They're just like our toys," Andrew said. "There's a clay pig that's really a rattle. And there are clay tops. And marbles made of glass. And a little wooden chariot with wheels that turn. And games." Andrew thought a minute. "And dolls," he added.

"I'd like to go the the British Museum," Timmie said.

But Andrew said, "The Science Museum is much nicer."

"What do they have *there?*" Timmie asked.

"Well, Tim," Daddy said, "let's go and see."

So Timmie and Andrew and Mother and Daddy all went to the Science Museum.

And as soon as they got there, Andrew said, "Let's go see 'Puffing Billy.'"

He ran through the Museum. Timmie ran after him. And Timmie thought he saw a locomotive.

He went closer.

He *did* see a locomotive. And it *was* "Puffing Billy," the first steam locomotive ever built.

She wasn't at all like the new locomotives Timmie had seen.

To Timmie, "Puffing Billy" looked more like a big barrel on a small wooden platform than an engine. But once upon a time she had gone clickety-clack along the tracks, pulling a wagon filled with coal.

Timmie and Andrew stared at "Puffing Billy" until Daddy led them to another room.

It was filled with locomotives, too. But they weren't nearly so big as "Puffing Billy." They were only models. Still, they were much, much larger than the American Flyer Timmie had found next to the bulging stocking at the foot of his bed last Christmas.

They were all in glass cases, just like the toys at the British Museum, so no one could touch them. But on the outside of the cases were buttons that you were *supposed* to touch, and handles that you were *supposed* to turn.

So Timmie and Andrew pushed the buttons.

And valves opened and closed and weights went up and down and pistons pushed rods and little wheels went around and made big wheels roll.

Andrew and Timmie turned a handle and a little train tootled off down the tracks to the end of the line at the end of the case.

They turned the handle the other way and the little engine backed up.

And after they pushed every button and turned every handle in the huge hall, they looked through a big glass window at a small room filled with old-fashioned tools. It was just like the workshop where James Watt, who developed the steam engine, had worked.

Timmie and Andrew might have stayed at the workshop all day, if Timmie hadn't noticed the cars in the large hall near by.

Some were very old and some were very new.

Some cars were very large and some were teeny, tiny ones.

The old cars were high and square and clumsy. And even though they had motors, they looked more like carriages that horses might pull. Hardly any had real windows. Hardly any even had tops.

The new cars, of course, were very different.

They were long and low and sleek, and very beautiful. Timmie was sure they would go faster than the

wind. They were the ones he would have liked to drive.

After they'd seen the cars, Timmie and Andrew and Mother and Daddy went upstairs to the rooms full of ships. These were models, too, like the ones they had seen in Greenwich. But there were many more of them.

There were tiny ice boats, and tiny seven-masted schooners.

There were rowboats and skiffs to sail on rivers.

There were birchbark canoes like those the Indians made, and kayaks like those the Eskimos used.

There were boats from Africa that were hardly more than rafts. There were small junks from China, and a large one with bamboo sails. There was a Chinese houseboat, carved in ivory.

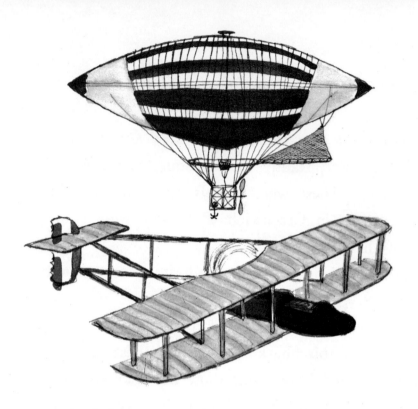

And there was a tiny sampan, built for passengers.
It had a cabin lined with mirrors. Inside the cabin
were tiny tables, with the tiniest tea sets Timmie had
ever seen. Timmie was trying to count the cups when
Andrew said, "They have planes, too."

He hurried over to the stairs. Timmie followed
right behind. And Mother and Daddy followed them
both.

But not right behind, of course. They were so far
behind that Timmie and Andrew had reached the
top floor and scurried through two galleries and down
a hall before Mother and Daddy caught up with
them.

But when they did, Timmie and Andrew were

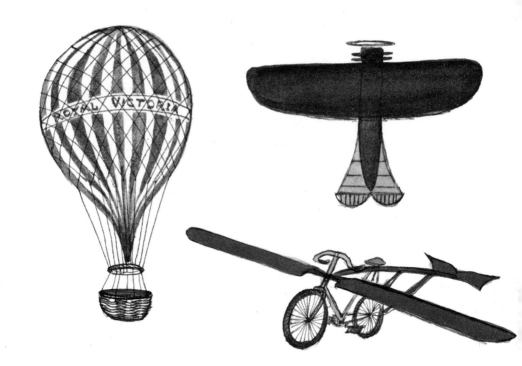

standing in front of a very frail, very small plane.

It was a copy of the *Kitty Hawk,* and it was *exactly* like the plane that Orville and Wilbur Wright had built, and that had been the first plane anyone ever flew in.

Right near it were other planes. Like the *Kitty Hawk,* they were life-size. But these weren't copies. The Spitfire Timmie and Andrew stared at was a real Spitfire. The Messerschmitt was too. Almost all the racing planes and almost all the warplanes and almost all the *modern* planes were real.

But the old-fashioned planes were only tiny models, that had been put together out of silk and wire and bamboo.

They were all arranged so that Timmie and Andrew could see how planes had been made bigger and better, and safer, too, from the time of the *Kitty Hawk* to those of today that cross oceans in a few hours.

There were other things, too.

There were wings men had worn when they tried to fly like birds. There were balloons with lovely orange-and-yellow, or blue-and-gold stripes. Little open baskets decorated with tiny flags hung beneath them. And in the baskets were tiny figures.

Long, long ago, men had really ridden in baskets like these, under balloons like these. They had been lifted high in the air and had floated through it. They had risked their lives to find out if such things could be done.

Near the balloons, Timmie and Andrew found parachutes. And Autogiros. And helicopters with propellers above them.

Then they found the cockpit of a Comet that was big enough to climb into.

Very carefully, Timmie and Andrew examined the dials with the pointers that looked like clocks, and the little lights, and the gauges. Timmie sighed at how much he would have to learn, if he were ever to fly a jet.

Just then, Daddy looked at his watch. "Goodness," he said, "it's already time for tea."

So they had their tea, right in the Museum. While they ate, Andrew told Timmie about the *other* science museum, the Natural History Museum, which was just around the corner. They had skeletons of dinosaurs there, the gigantic beasts that had roamed the earth millions of years ago. They had all kinds of other animals, too. They had herds of stuffed elephants, and a great stuffed whale. They had rare birds and rare fish. They even had a coelacanth, the oldest fish ever known. Andrew said the Natural History Museum had been the first place in the world to have one.

When they'd finished their tea, Daddy looked at his watch again. "I'm afraid it's time to go," he said.

They all went down the stairs, as slowly as possible, now, so that they could see everything . . . well, not everything . . . but so that they could still see *some* things.

In the big entrance hall, Timmie took Mother's hand, and Andrew took Daddy's. They all went outdoors.

Above them, the sky was blue and clear. The sun was shining brightly.

Timmie blinked. Mother shaded her eyes. "What a lovely day," she said.

Timmie sighed. He was as contented as his little kitten. "Yes," he said. "What a *lovely* day!"

7

The Houses of Parliament

Timmie and Andrew waited outside the hotel for Mother and Daddy. They were very impatient.

They were impatient because they were excited.

And they were excited because they were going to the Houses of Parliament.

Timmie had seen the great immense building when he and Mother and Daddy and Andrew had gone to Greenwich. It overlooked the Thames, just

across from the pier where they had taken the little boat.

Timmie thought it was the biggest building he had ever seen. When he told Daddy that, Daddy had said, "It's the biggest building *I've* ever seen, Tim. It has a hundred staircases in it, and more than a thousand rooms."

Timmie had stared at the high, square towers, with all the smaller towers at the corners and had watched the enormous hands of the clock that was set in still another tower. And then when Big Ben, the chimes in the clock, had struck the hour, Timmie had set his own watch by it.

Timmie had seen the Parliament building from the outside. But today was special. Today, Timmie and Andrew and Mother and Daddy were going inside.

On their way there Daddy told Timmie about it.

Sometimes, he said, people called the Houses of Parliament Westminster Palace, and once kings and queens had lived in it. Even though they didn't, now, they were still crowned in Westminster Abbey, just across the street.

Timmie thought someone ought to live in the Houses of Parliament still, if it were a house. But Daddy said no one did. It was just the place where the Members of Parliament went, to make the laws for all of Britain. "The way the American Congress meets in the Capitol building, in Washington," Daddy explained.

Timmie remembered then that part of Congress was called a House, too. It was the House of Representatives. But there was a second part of Congress, the Senate. So Timmie asked if there were two sections in Parliament, too.

And Daddy said yes. "There's the House of Commons, and the House of Lords."

Then Timmie wanted to know if the Members of Parliament were elected, the way they were in America.

Daddy said that everyone in the House of Commons was elected. "But the Lords have the right to help make the laws because their fathers or grandfathers or great-grandfathers did."

Then Daddy told Timmie about the Speaker's Procession. It took place every day Parliament was in session.

On those days, and just at half-past two, the Speaker of the House of Commons, with two men ahead, and two behind, marched through the halls.

They wore wonderful suits with knee breeches, and black stockings and polished black pumps with silver buckles. The Speaker wore a black robe over his suit. And he wore a white wig, too, that hung well below his shoulders.

But the wig looked more like tightly twisted rope than like hair.

The Serjeant at Arms, who walked ahead of the Speaker, carried a heavy gold staff. It was called "The Mace" and showed that the Speaker had the authority to preside over the House of Commons and keep order there.

As the procession went by, a bobby called out "Speaker" and another called out "Hats off, strangers." And, of course, everyone obeyed him.

On special days, like the day the Queen herself came to open Parliament . . . well, on special days, Daddy said, the Speaker wore a long robe with a train so long he had to have a trainbearer to carry it, like an Emperor in a fairy tale.

And on *extra* special occasions, like a Coronation, the Speaker rode in his own gold coach. It was drawn by a pair of handsome horses, and driven by a coachman in cocked hat and livery, cracking a long whip.

The Queen had a golden coach, too, even more beautiful than the Speaker's coach. When she rode in it, the Yeomen of the Guard walked beside it. They wore their blazing scarlet uniforms in her honor. And the Guards of the Household Cavalry marched ahead, wearing dark blue tail coats and white breeches and high black boots.

When the Queen opened Parliament, she rode from Buckingham Palace in her coach, and she was met by the Great Officers of State, who formed a procession and escorted her up the Royal Staircase to the Queen's Robing Room.

And when Timmie and Andrew and Mother and
Daddy reached Parliament, *they* went up to the
Robing Room, too.

Timmie thought the Robing Room belonged in a
fairy tale.

The walls were paneled in dark, dark wood. The
ceiling was as high as the sky and glittering with
golden beams. And all around the room were paintings of King Arthur and the Knights of the Round
Table. Under the paintings were wood carvings. And
they were of King Arthur and the Knights, too.

There was a chair of gold and ruby-red velvet on a red-carpeted platform at one end of the room. Timmie knew it was the Queen's because of the crown perched on top of it. And Daddy said that the large, lacy letters on the back showed that the chair had been made for Queen Victoria.

Over the chair was a golden canopy, carved with the symbols of the realm. There were roses for England and a thistle for Scotland and a shamrock for Ireland. On the tapestry behind the chair, a lion with a crown on his head growled at a unicorn. It was all so beautiful, Timmie was sure that this was the throne.

But Daddy said it wasn't. "It's beautiful," he agreed. And then he added, "We'll see the throne later."

Before they did, though, they went through the Royal Gallery. It was beautiful, too . . . so beautiful that Timmie blinked when he saw it.

The room glittered with gold, and gilded statues of kings and queens guarded the doors. And windows of stained glass spilled spots of color on a floor laid out in polished patterns, and lit up the paintings on the walls. Timmie and Andrew walked around the room. And it was such a big room that that took a very long time.

They looked at the enormous painting on one wall which showed the Duke of Wellington. He was a great hero because he had defeated the French at Waterloo.

They looked at the enormous painting of Lord Nelson on another wall. He had been an admiral. And he had defeated the French and Spanish fleets in a famous battle at Trafalgar.

And then, before they saw the throne, they went through the Prince's Chamber. There were pictures of kings and queens and princes on the walls, and right away, Timmie recognized Henry VIII. And Daddy pointed out all six of King Henry's wives.

At the end of the room was a gleaming white statue of Queen Victoria, the Queen for whom the Chair of State had been made. She had been Queen of all Great Britain . . . of England and Scotland and Wales. She had been Queen of Ireland, too, and Empress of India. Queen Victoria had ruled for more than sixty years. During that time, England had become rich and powerful.

After they'd seen the Prince's Chamber, Timmie and Andrew and Mother and Daddy went into the Chamber of the House of Lords. That was where the Lords discussed new laws and voted on them.

And *that* was where Timmie saw the throne.

Behind another Chair of State, the wall was all of gold, as dazzling as the brightest sunlight. Golden panels reached halfway to the ceiling, and the ceiling was the highest Timmie had ever seen.

The golden panels reached far to each side, too. Daddy said that chairs were placed in front of them for other members of the Royal Family when the Queen spoke to Parliament.

It was like . . . well, it *wasn't* like anything Timmie had ever seen before. It wasn't like anything he would ever see again. It was more splendid, it was more beautiful, than the throne of any king or queen or prince in any fairy tale.

Even though Timmie could have reached out his hand and touched it . . . he didn't, of course . . . it seemed like something in a dream.

After they'd seen the throne, Timmie and Andrew and Mother and Daddy went on through the other rooms. Some had great soaring stone arches. Some were paneled in polished wood. Some were filled with statues and some with paintings.

But Timmie hardly noticed. All he could think of was the great golden throne.

Even when they reached Westminster Hall, with the broad steps like the layers in a wedding cake that led down to the stained glass window, Timmie hardly noticed.

And he didn't really listen when Daddy told him about King Charles I, who had lived long ago, and had tried to take away the liberties that the Magna Charta guaranteed to the English people. Because of that, King Charles had been condemned to death, right in the hall Timmie was standing in.

England had been ruled by Oliver Cromwell, then, who was called the "Lord Protector." But later, the son of King Charles, who became King Charles II, had regained the throne. And he had condemned to death the judges who had condemned his father.

Timmie didn't even think about King Charles until he got back to the hotel. Then he remembered something he had seen back home, in Guilford.

It was a sign on a cellar, almost next door to the house Timmie lived in. It said that two of the judges who had decided King Charles must die had hidden . . . right in that cellar . . . for three days, while the new King's men were looking for them.

When Timmie thought about the throne again, it didn't seem like a dream.

It seemed very real.

And England didn't seem to be a foreign country at all.

Even if there *was* an ocean between them, Timmie knew that America and England were really very close.

8

…and Home

The days were getting chilly. When Timmie went down to wait for the milkman, he always put his sweater on. Sometimes he put his coat on, too.

The kitten was getting bigger.

She still drank her cream politely. She still fell asleep on Timmie's lap at times. But she never played with the string he dangled in front of her any more. She was too grown up.

And the days were getting shorter. It was barely light, now, when Timmie went down to feed the kitten.

Timmie's time in London was getting shorter, too.

Mother and Daddy were busy making plans for going home. They were busy packing. They were busy with last-minute shopping and with last-minute visits.

One day Timmie complained, "But there's still so much to see. Do you think we'll ever see it all?"

"Oh, dear, no," Mother said. She and Timmie and Andrew all stopped to look at polished leather handbags in a window. "Not even half."

"Maybe a quarter?" Timmie asked hopefully.

Mother laughed and took Timmie's hand in one of hers. She took Andrew's hand in the other. "I don't know. But we can still see *something*."

"What?" Timmie asked.

"Oh, dear," Mother said. "I don't know." And then, the way mothers sometimes do, she said, "We'll go to Kensington Gardens. We'll go there now."

So Timmie and Andrew and Mother hopped on the very next bus that came along.

They had hardly paid their fares before they passed a building that Timmie knew was a church because of the cross on top.

It was very big, and very beautiful, with a round dome in the center and twin towers on the sides. It was built up, with one level on top of another. And each level was decorated with slim, straight columns.

Timmie turned to look at the building. Mother turned to look at it, too. And Andrew said, "That's St. Paul's."

Then Timmie remembered that he had seen the dome of St. Paul's Cathedral before. It had been the day they sailed down the Thames, and Daddy had pointed it out to him. That was when Daddy had told Timmie about Sir Christopher Wren, who had designed the Cathedral.

But Daddy hadn't told Timmie about the big, broad square that they came to in almost no time at all.

At one end of the square was a small white church with a delicate spire and graceful columns.

And there was a museum, too. There were museums *everywhere* in London.

Mother said this was the National Museum and that it was filled with famous old paintings and statues. They had been brought to London from all parts of the world.

The building was so big . . . it was so long and so wide . . . that Timmie thought there must have been millions and millions of paintings and statues inside. Mother said there certainly were thousands and thousands.

But it wasn't because of the Museum that Timmie said, "Let's get off here!"

It wasn't because of the church, either.

It was because of the tall column near the front of the square with the statue of Lord Nelson at the top of it. It was because of the four bronze lions ly-

ing in wait at the foot of the column, as if they were
ready to pounce. And it was because of the two
bright pools of water with a fountain plashing and
splashing in the center of each of them.

Timmie had no sooner said it than he and Andrew
were scampering to the back of the bus and dashing
down the stairs. They jumped off while the man who
had taken their tickets was still calling out "Trafalgar Square."

Timmie knew that Trafalgar was the place off the
coast of Spain where Lord Nelson had won his great
sea victory, because he had seen the picture of the

Battle of Trafalgar, in the Houses of Parliament. And he knew that the Square had been named in honor of that.

As soon as they'd jumped off the bus, Timmie and Andrew rushed off to the fountains. They watched as the water sprayed high in the air and spilled back into the fountains and flowed over the edges of them, as white and foamy and frothy as the embroidery on the curtains in Mother's room back home.

When they were tired of looking at the

big fountains, Timmie and Andrew walked around one of the pools to look at a smaller one. It was made of bronze, and had the head and body of a beautiful woman, and the tail of a fish, and Andrew said it was a mermaid.

After that, they went back to Mother. She was standing in the center of Trafalgar Square, with plump, pearly-gray pigeons all around her feet. The pigeons were so tame that Timmie could almost have touched them. He certainly could have touched them if he'd had food for them.

So Mother gave Timmie and Andrew some pennies and they ran off to buy corn from the woman who sold little containers of it right there.

Then, when Timmie held out the corn, the pigeons strutted up to him and ate it right out of his hand.

When the pigeons had eaten every single grain of corn and had fluttered away, Mother said it was time to go. "If we want to get to Kensington Gardens," she added.

They left Trafalgar Square, then, and crossed the street. They walked through a small archway set, like the very large archways, right into the building that curved like the new moon across the broadest street Timmie had ever seen. Straight ahead, at the end of the street, was Buckingham Palace.

They all walked toward it, but before they reached it, Andrew said, "Look! There's St. James's Palace."

It was very big and very old, and made of red brick with white bricks to trim it. There was a jagged wall around the roof, and there were turrets and towers almost everywhere.

They all stopped beside the Palace. Mother said that it had been built for Henry VIII. Now it was the place where the Queen Mother lived.

They were still standing near St. James's Palace when Andrew said "Listen!"

Then from far away, Timmie heard a band playing. He and Andrew turned around. And coming up the street from Buckingham Palace was a regiment of Guards.

Timmie and Andrew hurried along to the iron gates of St. James's Palace. The Guards reached the gates and swung around and marched into the Palace grounds just as Timmie and Andrew got there. So they watched until the Guards disappeared. They listened until the music had faded away.

Then they got on another bus. They didn't get off at Kensington Gardens, though. They got off near a long, narrow lake called the Serpentine that wound through Hyde Park.

They crossed the green grass to a little boathouse on the lake. They got into one of the little rowboats that bobbed up and down on the water. And Timmie and Andrew rowed until they saw a statue at the end of the lake—in Kensington Gardens.

As soon as they saw it, Timmie and Andrew knew who it was. Together they said, "It's Peter Pan!"

"Yes," Mother said. "It's Peter Pan."

Timmie could remember the whole story. Daddy had read it all to him at bedtime back in America.

Andrew could remember the story, too. Andrew's Daddy had read *Peter Pan* to Andrew just at bedtime here in England.

That night, after Timmie had climbed into bed and pulled the covers up to his chin, and the kitten had jumped on the bed and curled up at Timmie's feet, Daddy read part of *Peter Pan* to Timmie again.

And the next day . . . well, the next day it was time for Timmie to say good-by to Andrew. Not for just a few days, this time. It was time to say good-by because Timmie and Mother and Daddy were going back to America. They were going back to Timmie's Guilford.

But before they did, they went out to Andrew's Guildford.

Just as Timmie and Mother and Daddy were leaving their hotel, the kitten came around the corner. She padded over to Timmie and said, "Me-ow."

Timmie scooped her up in his arms. "Daddy," he asked, "what about my kitten?"

Daddy looked very thoughtful. "I don't know, Tim," he said.

"I can't leave her here alone," Timmie said.

"No," Mother said, "you can't leave her here alone."

"And you *really* can't take her back to America," Daddy said.

"No," Timmie said. "I guess I can't."

"Why don't you take her to Guildford?" Mother asked. "Why don't you leave your kitten with Andrew?"

So Timmie and Mother went to a little shop and bought a basket to carry the kitten in. And when Mother and Daddy and Timmie went to Guildford, the kitten went along, too.

All the way there, Timmie didn't say anything. He was thinking.

Timmie was thinking about all the things that were the same at home in America as here in England.

He was thinking of the language he and Andrew both spoke.

He was thinking of the laws they both obeyed.

He was thinking of the way those laws were made, and of Parliament and of Congress.

And he was thinking of Andrew's daddy reading

Peter Pan to Andrew, just the way Daddy read it to him.

Andrew was waiting for Timmie and Mother and Daddy in Guildford. Together, he and Timmie carried the kitten in her basket into his house.

When they opened the basket, the kitten jumped out. She stretched and said, "Me-ow." Then she hopped up on a chair and curled up. She began to purr.

She seemed to feel quite at home.

It was just the way Timmie had felt, all the time in England . . . quite at home.

It was just the way Timmie felt now . . . as if he had come from Guildford.

And in a way he had.

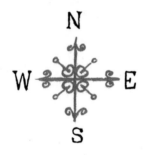

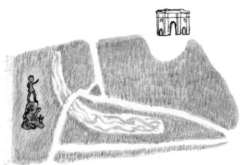

Hyde Park

Buckingham Palace

Science Museum

TO GUILDFORD, 30 miles

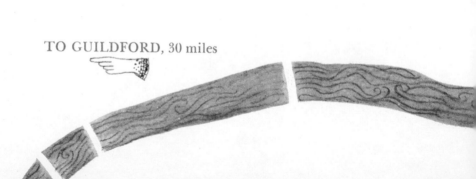

Nelson Monument

St. Paul's
Cathedral

Tower of
London

The Monument

Tower
Bridge

TO GREENWICH

...es of
...ament

TIMMIE'S LONDON

About the Author

Vivian Werner was born in Bellingham, Washington, grew up in Seattle, and attended Bennington College in Vermont, where she majored in music. As a free-lance journalist now living in Paris, Mrs. Werner's career has included the writing of radio scripts, advertising copy, and magazine articles as well as books. Her first adult novel, *The Breaking Wave*, published in England, was the British nomination for the Prix Formentor of 1961.

Mrs. Werner made her first trip to London with her two sons, who were then eight and six years old, and much of her book is based on her experiences with them. She has since been to England many times and made three trips for research on *Timmie in London*.

Mrs. Werner's first book for children, *Timmie in Paris*, was published in 1965.

About the Artist

Elise Piquet has been, among other things, an art teacher, an art director for a major publishing house, a magazine illustrator, and an advertising artist. *Timmie in Paris* was the first *book* she illustrated. Miss Piquet lives in New York City, and when not busy at her drawing board, she collects antiques.